Hello Kitty's
Pet Puppy

By Rachel Lisberg
Illustrated by Sachiho Hino

SCHOLASTIC INC.

New York   Toronto   London   Auckland   Sydney
Mexico City   New Delhi   Hong Kong   Buenos Aires

Decorate the pictures in this book with stickers. The page numbers on the sticker pages will help you figure out which stickers to use.

ISBN-13: 978-0-439-87139-6
ISBN-10: 0-439-87139-5

12 11 10 9 8 7 6 5 4 3 2   9 10 11 12/0

Printed in the U.S.A.
First printing, January 2007

Hello Kitty opened her eyes.
It was Saturday.
Today was the day she was getting her
new puppy!

Hello Kitty had always wanted a puppy.
Mama and Papa said having a puppy was
a lot of work.

But now they thought she was ready to
take care of one by herself.

Hello Kitty and Mimmy played a game
while they waited for Papa.
He had gone out to pick up the new
puppy.

They couldn't wait till he got home!

"Can I help you brush the puppy?"
Mimmy asked Hello Kitty.
"Of course, Mimmy," Hello Kitty said.
"It will be your puppy, too. Just like you
let me help take care of your fish."

Just then they heard Papa at the door.
He came in holding a big brown box.
"Oh! Put it down so we can see!" Hello
Kitty squealed.

Inside there was a tiny white puppy with
a big black spot over one eye.
"He's so cute!" said Hello Kitty. "I think
I'm going to name him Spotty!"

There was a lot to do.
First Hello Kitty showed Spotty where
his bed and food bowls were.

Then she showed him how to walk on
a leash.
She even began to teach him how to sit!

Hello Kitty was so busy that she forgot
to call her friends!
She had promised to tell them the puppy's
name.
Then the phone rang.

"It's for you, Hello Kitty," Mama said. "It's Fifi. She wants to know how it's going with your new puppy!"

Hello Kitty told Fifi about Spotty.
"Can I come over later to see him?"
Fifi asked.
"That would be great," Hello Kitty
said.

Then she looked down.
"Uh-oh! I have to go!" she told Fifi.
"Spotty just chewed up a newspaper!"

When the doorbell rang, Hello Kitty ran
to greet her friends.
Tracy and Tippy came, too.
Everyone brought Spotty gifts!

There were bones, chew toys, and a welcome sign.
"Ruff, ruff!" barked Spotty happily as he wagged his tail.

After Spotty played with his gifts it was
time for him to eat.
Hello Kitty told Tippy what to do.

"He's really hungry!" Tippy said.
"Puppies are always hungry," Hello Kitty
said. "They grow really fast so they eat
a lot!"

When Spotty finished, he had food on his face and paws.
"We should give him a bath," Fifi said.
They took turns scrubbing Spotty clean.

"Quick! Grab the towel!" Hello Kitty said.
It was too late.
"I guess we took a bath, too!" Fifi said.

After everyone dried off, Tracy had
an idea.
"Let's go outside to teach Spotty to
fetch!" he said.

The friends put on their coats and hats.
Hello Kitty picked up Spotty.

The friends took turns throwing a stick
for Spotty.
He was a fast learner!
Tracy threw the stick far.

Spotty ran off to catch it, but he didn't come back.
"Uh-oh!" said Hello Kitty. "Where did Spotty go?"

They looked under the trees.
They looked behind the shovel.
They called his name.

But they could not find Spotty!
"What if Spotty is lost forever?" Hello
Kitty cried.

Then Hello Kitty thought she saw
something.
A black rock on the ground looked
like it moved.

Then it moved again!

It wasn't a rock at all!
It was the black spot over Spotty's eye!
Spotty was caught in a snowbank!
His white fur made him hard to see.

The friends quickly dug Spotty out.
Hello Kitty gave her puppy a big hug.

"We should take Spotty inside to get warm," Hello Kitty said.
"Yes, let's hurry," Mimmy said.

Papa made everyone hot cocoa.
Mama gave Spotty a bright red collar.
"I love you so much, Spotty!" Hello Kitty
said. "Now we'll never lose you again!"